Serenade of Currents

Slow Burn Romance Fantasy

Heidi McLynn

Heidi McLynn

Contents

Chapter One -
Song Of Chains

♥

I run my fingers through the blue water basin at my bedside, and feel the water's strength enter my fingertips, even as an unsettled feeling pushes against my ribcage. I want to scrub the unsettled feeling away, but it stays like a burr under my skin.

My mother, the Queen, stands behind me, pulling the brush through my long, silky black hair. I may be beautiful, with unblemished skin, deep green eyes, and a perfect smile that can lure any man, yet she is gorgeous as ever; her pure Siren beauty unrelenting as the sun.

"You will marry Prince Kurt tomorrow, tomorrow, you'll marry him tomorrow!" she chants, her eyes glittering. My mother's voice is exuberant, smooth as silk, and tempting as dark chocolate.

For other daughters, in other lands, a mother's song might be a wonderful thing, but for me, it is not so. I try to muster up the will to fight back. I try to put up some invisible shield, as I've seen my mother do, time and again. Try as I might, her voice cuts through my flesh and takes up residence in my bones.

"No, I won't, I won't, I won't, I won't!" I manage to sing back, not even sure where I find the strength.

She turns toward me, and she smiles, her perfect lips revealing perfect teeth. Everything about her looks perfect, from her vibrant auburn hair that flows to her waist, to her curved hips and glossy skin. That is how we Sirens are, although I am only half-Siren. The other half, my human half, my mother tells me, is weak, and stupid. I do not agree. I believe even humans can be strong.

"Yes, you will, you will," she sings, until I can only nod. The perfect, obedient daughter. The daughter I despise is the daughter I am, once again.

Tomorrow, I tell myself. Tomorrow, I will be stronger. Tomorrow, I will run away, and never look back.

When I wake the next morning, I tell myself I am not going to let her control me, not in this. I can withstand being told what to wear. I am able to deal with her telling me how to eat, and how to curtsy, and how to be a proper lady, but not this. I will do anything to stay as far from love as possible. Even if I would dare to dream of true love, I know true love can never have the likes of me. Every man is in love with my appearance, and my voice. I cannot expect anything better than this, being what I am. I saw the look on Prince Kurt's face three nights ago. He was under the Siren spell; he doesn't love me, not the real me.

I pull on my boots, slip into a riding dress, pack food from the kitchen, and grab my brother's old sword, though I have no idea how to use it. It is all I can do to drag myself out of the back door of the castle and toward the edge of the Wood, pulling myself inch by inch, struggling for air all the way. My mother is not far behind. I can hear her song reaching for me, like dark tentacles of the sea. I resist. I breathe. I think of a song pure and lovely, and somehow, as if by a miracle, I reach the edge of the Wood, where soft grass turns to dirt, thorns and flowers.

My dress is dirty, but it no longer matters. I can stand up. I can run. I am free. I step into the Wood, feeling that I am finally on my own adventure. Not an adventure picked by my mother, but my very own. These are steps to be cherished. These are moments I will remember forever. This is the moment when I, Princess Eloise, am becoming my own woman.

I want to dance, or to sing among the green leaves of the Wood, but I am not completely unaware that this is one of the most dangerous places on our island. A place that only the bravest hunters ever dared to enter, for there is said to live here the most despicable hostile mobs on earth: undead skeletons, exploding creepers, and worst of all, the three-headed Wither. My mother has said how uncontrollable the mobs are, and if she cannot control them, then no one can.

I crouch down and proceed on my hands on knees, ignoring the scraping of branches against my knees, not wanting to be noticed by anyone, not that this will help. Back home, everyone noticed me. For my beauty and my voice. I've seen how my mother uses her voice to control others, and I vowed I'd never use my power, not in the same way she does.

An arrow zings past my right ear, grazing it. I bite back a yelp, and fall to my face. Right now would be the time I could really use my voice. Right now I need to use it, for my own survival. I don't think, but I open my mouth and sing my song.

"Leave me be, leave me be, leave me be," I sing, over and over again, but the arrows do not desist in their coming. It isn't working, but of course. They must be immune to my song. They are powerful indeed. A Siren's song is as powerful as the strongest potion, and yet it has no power over these creatures. I crouch behind a large tree and think of the sea. Water always makes me feel safe, no matter where I am, and this time when I think of the sea, it arrives in great waves, standing tall as a wall beside me. I gaze at the beautiful colors, forgetting my danger, until I hear the whiz of arrows once more. The arrows stick to the water, as if the water were a barrier between me and my enemies. How can this be? I smile and put my hand into the water. "I am grateful," I say, speaking to the water, and it pushes back against my hand, as if it understands.

I know from the survival books at the castle that one is to build a shelter to keep the mobs at bay. I don't know how long the water will protect me, nor how the sea magic works. I begin to build myself a shelter from the trees all around me.

My father desired for me to be prepared, but he never imagined I'd ever need to fight. Fighting is not something princesses are allowed to do, but now that I've come to this place, my days as a Princess are over. I thought I would be glad. Once, I envied my brother. I envied his ability to do what he chose, but now that he has passed, I only feel sorrow. The water recedes, returning to whence it came. I am sad to see it go, but I know I cannot keep it forever. That is the way the sea is. It goes where it will.

Darkness comes swiftly, and my hands tremble as I place the last blocks for the ceiling into place. I am not quick enough, and the whoosh of zinging arrows are heard above my head and all around. I duck inside my shelter. Looking up, I see that there's one block-width space to fill and I don't have enough wood.

I crouch down on the floor. I can go back out, and risk death by arrows, or wait for the mobs to find the missing hole. I poke my head through the door, peering out into the darkness, hoping the mobs have left.

Not hearing anything, I dart to the nearest tree, punch down one more block, then tiptoe back toward my door, only to find my way blocked. A skeleton towers over me, his bow ready, a sharp arrow pointed at my head.

Everything is frozen in place. Even if I pull out my sword now, I won't be quick enough. If I try to fight him, it will end in my death.

"Please," I say, "Let me. live." My breath is ragged. My voice holds no power here, and even when I think of the sea, there is no watery wall to protect me now. I don't have time, and yet death has all the time in the world.

I wait. Sweat gathers under my collar, and my fingers itch, touching the cold blade of my sword. A sword I have no idea how to use. Something my brother left for me. A moment later, I see a shadow, and I feel the comforting presence of the water once again. *Will it protect me now, just as it did earlier?* Without a word, the skeleton melts into the shadow.

My body trembles as I rush through my door and let it close with a sigh of relief. I shove the last block in place. When I lie down on my bed, I wonder if sleep will ever come. Every noise reminds me of skeletons and creepers.

I jump at every rustle, expecting something to break through at any moment. But what confuses me the most is the skeleton. *He didn't simply take my life, but why? Why did he choose mercy?* After all, our people haven't treated the skeletons with any more kindness than one would show a wild dog. And as I've been taught by my mother and all of the kingdom, this is just what they deserve.

Chapter Two - Tied Up

♥

When I wake, all is quiet. I wonder where I am. My head aches, but when I get up and peek out of the crack in the door, everything rushes back. I wish it were not so.

The Wood appears calm and too quiet in the daylight, as if everything has finally gone to sleep. The tree leaves are a shimmering green, and there are beautiful yellow, orange, and pink flowers coating the forest floor. I bend down to examine a pink flower at my feet, but I know I have to keep my guard up. There could still be mobs here, waiting and watching in the shadows.

The first matter of business is food. I search the area for edibles. Having been required to learn herbology under my tutor, I know the plants well, and quickly find some flowers I can eat. I munch on these, yet it would be nice to have a cup of milk, or maybe some meat. Those things won't come easily, so for now, some flowers will have to do. My stomach grumbles in protest at this meager meal.

I walk a few yards from my hut, and hear something in the bushes. Is someone watching me? Or something?

I'm surprised to find a skeleton walk out, in broad daylight, and stand only a few feet away from me. He doesn't raise up his bow, or seem to be out for an attack, which is odd. Is there something wrong with the skeletons around here? Why isn't he burning up?

The skeleton laughs, unsettling me, his laugh like fingers running across a rough piece of bark.

"What be a human princess doing in the middle of this place?" he says.

Is it wise to speak to one of his kind?

"That is my own matter," I say. How can I explain why I ran from home? That I didn't wish to be controlled any longer. That I ran from my own family.

I must make friends with these strange creatures, no matter what they have done. My life depends on it. I feel a jerk on my ankles, as my body is flipped upside down. I shriek. I'm hanging upside down by my ankles, the odd skeleton smiling at me, like a thief proud of his spoils. I could die in mere minutes. I have to act quickly.

"Anyone who travels these parts must state their business, especially one of your kind," he says. It looks like he's grinning down at me. "Now tell me what a pampered siren Princess be doing in these parts."

I turn and twist, trying to find a way to untie myself. I open my mouth and sing, "Release Me!" but the skeleton shakes his skull. He is one of those creatures who can't be controlled, unfortunately. I think of the sea, but nothing happens, and I don't have time to wait for it to respond. I don't even know how Sea Magic works, or if it came to me because I had a real need.

"I'm running from home. Seeking safety from those who wish to control me," I say. "Now, kindly release me..." I stop speaking mid-sentence when my body falls toward the ground. I crumple to the soft earth, attempting a gentle roll. There are stabbing pains in my neck.

I stand up, stretch my neck, and wipe the dirt from my face with my handkerchief that no longer resembles anything close to the color white. I scan the clearing. The skeleton is still here. He relaxes against a tree, his face uplifted toward the sun. His bony figure is kind of sad, with all of its rough edges and gray bones and the thin gray smile. He slaps his bone fingers together and they make a clacking noise.

"Now, you'll be needing to learn some rules," he says. "Firstly, no killing trees."

"How do I stay safe at night? How do I build shelters? Make fires?" I ask, the questions running out of my mouth one after another. Without a shelter, the mobs will attack me. Turn me to dust in moments. Without fire, I won't survive the winter.

"Once you kill tree, there's no safety," he says, gazing upwards. "We be guardians of tree, plant and animal. You be thankful yer still alive wee one. Now, tell me, who was trying to control you?"

"My mother wished for me to marry," I say, turning away from him. "And she has the power to make me do whatever she likes." The words sound strange in my mouth. Like some sad line from someone else's story. I still don't know if I'm safe from her power.

"These woods aren't safe either, not for you," he says. "But ye already know that. Water blocks," he says, leading me to the edge of the island. "Mobs won't step foot into water."

I shake my head, and yet I remember how the water had protected me before. Maybe it isn't such a wild idea, but it seems so simple. So easy. Too easy.

"That's the problem with ye. Thinking ya know so much about us." He turns from me to face the watery bogs that surround us on every side and through the mist, several boats float past our small island. "Suit yerself, princess."

I take a breath of the misty air and gaze into the watery wood beyond, making sure to keep one eye on this skeleton. Is what he's telling me true? I have no way of knowing. No way except to make a choice and see what happens. Do I risk angering the trees and the skeletons who guard them, or follow his advice? In the distance I glimpse a boat headed toward the island. I take some blocks of water, and stack them on top of each other, until I have a shelter, yet it looks as foolish as one building their house out of straw.

"How was it, being a princess, living in that fancy castle?" the skeleton says.

When I think about life in the castle, I remember what it was like living in the cage of dos and don'ts. Of wrongs and rights. Of polite and impolite rules, and of every moment being ruled by someone else's voice. That was the most uncomfortable of all. Of course, I sang back, but my voice was never as powerful. It was never as beautiful or as strong.

"It's comfortable, but it's not nice. Not at all," I say.

"Yer a strange one," he says. "But the stranger, the better is what I always say." He steps closer while I take a step back. "Me name's Skully." He holds out his hand to me.

"What do you want from me?" I ask, starting to feel frightened. Starting to wonder why he doesn't leave me alone. I glance at the boat, still a ways off, and crouch down behind a bush.

"Want?" he says, as if this is a strange concept. "I only desire love. That be all."

"I've spent my life running from such mushy nonsense," I say, knowing that I could have anyone I chose. One of the curses of being

a siren or the daughter of a siren, is that everyone thinks you're beautiful..

"Why would one run from a thing of beauty?" asks Skully.

I shrug. I wanted to be able to do all the things men did. Hunt, and fight, and be strong. I wanted to be independent. I wish I weren't so beautiful. I wish I could blend in with everyone else. At least here, the skeletons don't care for beauty, or my song.

"The love I've seen wasn't beautiful," I reply.

He says, "I'm talking about the true kind of love. The kind that wins battles. The kind that comes from The One. The kind more powerful than magic of any kind."

The boat is nearing. I hurry into my watery shelter, watching the fish swim through the watery walls of my dwelling. The skeleton sits outside on the sand. On the boat, there are knights I once trusted to protect me. They are calling for me. *Eloise! Eloise! Eloise!* Do they mean harm or good? Do I reveal myself? I want to run to them more than anything, but the water whispers hush, hush, hush. If I go with them, I'll have to marry for sure.

Even as I sit and wait, I feel something rushing in my fingertips. A watery swelling that pushes itself up and out, so that the floor begins to be filled with water.

The Knights reach my dwelling. My own people. My heart aches.

Chapter Three – Followed

♥

S kully stands on the sands facing the crew, as if he can fight the whole lot of them. There are too many, but instead of attacking the skeleton, the leader steps up and talks to him as if he were a human being. As if he were just one of us.

"There's a bounty out for a princess. The Queen will give lands and protection to any who return the princess to her majesty, dead or alive."

Skully says, "I haven't seen her, but if I do, I'll return her to ya."

Why is the Queen offering to protect skeletons, those whom we are at war with? Those whom she hates with every part of her? Is she searching for me because she cares, or because she wants me to do as she likes?

I sit down slowly in my watery shell and wait for the men to pass by. If they search inside here, my life is over. The men walk by my shelter, as if it doesn't exist, and on-wards into the other parts of the island, but I know I'm not safe, not yet. As dusk nears, I hear Skully's sad music as he strums his fingers across his chest bones. I wait for him to turn into his true self: the evil skeleton. I wait for him to leave in search of blood, but I fall asleep to the music and do not wake until sunlight is pouring through my watery cocoon. I stretch and step outside to find Skully sleeping, his skull resting upon a stone.

"Time to wake up, lazy-bones," I call.

I step back as he rises. He only hums a tune and stretches. I can't help but wonder what he did last night. If he really was asleep all night, or if he destroyed lives while the rest of the world slept.

"Why didn't you tell them about me?" I say.

"The Queen be full of bad intentions," Skully says. "We cannot stay here."

"We?" I ask.

"Can't expect me to let ya have all the fun now, can we?" Skully asks.

And even though I fear him, I know that I am going to need a guide through these unknown lands. I just shake my head, and pack up my things.

"Well then, it's settled. We're going on an adventure," Skully says, rocking back on his heels, and gazing up at the sun. I would never guess he is a murderous skeleton, not by the way he looks right now, but I have to remember that he is a monster, no matter what he might appear to be under the light of the sun.

"Why do you kill?" I ask.

Skully scratches his skull with a long finger bone. "That's the horrible thing. Our evil side comes to life every night, until the curse be broken. Some embrace the curse and others resist it, still, it lives in each one of us."

I had heard of the curse, but always thought it was a fairy tale. A way to give the skeletons a reason for what they did. A way to make sense of things.

"I mean to break the curse," Skully says. "How?" I ask.

"I don't know, " he says."But it has to do with love, I can tell ye that."

Skully brings me to his metal boat, and I climb on board, hesitating for a moment before setting foot on his craft. This is the end. The end of the life I knew. We push off from the island, moving slowly between the majestic trees that seem to float upon the sparkling blue and green water. This place is beautiful, even with all its danger. Skully looks nervously down at the water.

"How can a pirate be afraid of water?" I ask.

He smiles back at me, "How can a princess fear her own castle?"

And I find myself smiling back, though I should not be talking to this creature at all.

I do not fear the water. Rather, it comforts me, the sound of it rushing under the boat, and when I reach down to touch it, I feel that everything is going to be alright, even if it isn't.

We reach another island before nightfall, and I am grateful, for I do not wish to see what Skully is like after dark, and I see the anxious glimmer in his black eye sockets, or maybe it's only a trick of the fading light.

I set up my shelter and once again I go inside, waiting for dark to come, and watching Skully, pacing in front of my dwelling, as his song begins, low and sad. The fear returns that he might attack. That maybe this watery abode is only a trick of his, but once again, the water lulls me to sleep, as if within its walls everything is alright, and I wake to a new day, still alive and Skully still there, waiting for me.

"Where does our path lead?" I ask, wondering where I'm to go from here. I wonder who I am, and I no longer know.

"For now we be avoid-in' the King's men," Skully says.

"How do we do that? For they have magic beyond any skill of mine," I ask.

"There be places even Knights won't venture," Skully says, "There be places."

I don't ask him what these places might be. If Knights won't go there, it cannot be a pleasant place. I hear a rustle in a thicket, and I feel as if something or someone is following us.

Chapter Four - Raft

♥

W e're being followed," I whisper.

Skully says, "Aye."

"And?" I say, "Who is it?"

"Why don't ye go check?" Skully says.

I glare at him. "I'm not checking. That would be madness."

"Then, I suggest we run," Skully says.

I scramble after him, up the hill and toward the raft. We heave ourselves aboard and continue on our way through the watery forest.

I turn around and glimpse a figure on shore. It plunges into the water and then disappears. I shiver and wrap my cloak tighter around myself.

"What was that?" I ask Skully.

"There be many mysteries, even I don't understand, ancient as I be," Skully says. "Some things are better left unanswered."

My stomach growls. "What is there to dine on?" I ask.

Skully says, "There's algae in the water. There's every kind of meat, if ye can get it and plants all around us, if ye know what's good and what's not."

"And if I don't know?" I ask.

"Then ye don't eat," he says, "That's the way it be."

"Teach me," I say, my stomach protesting. I'm so famished I'll eat anything.

Skully fishes out a clump of green gooey mess from the water and tosses it back to me. It lands with a slick, slimy glop on my boots.

I pick up the goo, and with a brave determination, I put one piece of green slime onto my tongue, and find that it tastes good in a strange, bitter sort of way. Or maybe I am just that hungry that anything tastes good.

I take another couple of bites and find that I am satisfied.

We pass another island. I glimpse the Knights' tunics, but too late. I duck down, but when I hear their shouts, I know they have spotted me. Arrows hit the sides of our raft, and I know that they do not intend to save my life.

Skully sends out an orangey blue fire on our raft, or at least I think it's coming from his fleshless fingers. I don't have time to wonder where it's coming from.

"Extinguish the flame!" I shout, "Do you mean to burn us to ashes?"

"Nothing of the sort, princess," he says, with a wink of one of his blackened eye sockets. "This be our protection."

He motions for me to sit behind the fire, but I shake my head and reach toward the water. Skully pulls me back with such force I'm sent flying onto my back.

"Look!" he says.

When I sit up, I am shocked to see that our raft is neither burning up nor singed.

"What kind of fire is this?" I ask.

"A kind that only a skeleton can make," he says. "Given to us by the trees. It only burns one's enemies and protects those we love."

"But how does fire understand such things?" I say, as I gaze upon the wall that stands between me and those who would capture us.

The fire dissipates a moment later, and we are far from the island, but now there is a new enemy on this raft. It is love. The one thing I've been successful in avoiding. Yet, even if Skully truly loves me, which I do not believe he can, at least I am in no danger of loving him.

The day is growing later, and I don't see any islands in sight. *How am I going to survive an entire night on a raft with a skeleton whose evil side comes out at night?*

"Is there any place to stop?" I ask.

Skully says, "There be no islands for miles."

"And what of the curse?" I ask.

"Let's hope ye can hold me at bay," Skully says, "Else ye may have to kill me."

"That isn't a joking matter," I say.

"I wasn't joking," he says.

I throw a stick in his direction, and one of his finger bones falls off.

"Now look," he says, a twinkle in his eye sockets, almost like the glimmer of a star.

"I don't wish to kill you," I say.

"I don't wish that either, but sometimes we be needing to do what we hate," Skully says.

I laugh, wondering how he can seem so relaxed about all of this. Of course, he is a skeleton, so death doesn't frighten him.

"I'll make a shelter on the boat," I say, wondering why I didn't think of this before.

"There isn't enough space on this tiny craft," Skully says, "But the water protects ye, Princess, and ye run to the trees if all else fails."

I nod and wait as the sun sinks lower in the sky. I desire to dive down into the water, but I don't know what lies underneath the dark, still surface. Skully's eyes change from black to inky black. His mouth twists into a downward spiral, and when he looks at me, it isn't the kind pirate I see, but a skeleton awoken from the dead.

"Lord save me," I whisper, and I reach my hand down into the water, willing it to come to my aid, asking it to help me, but I hear no answer, and I do not even feel the water stir beneath my fingertips.

I do not wish to kill this creature. This one who has been there to protect me, and yet, as he advances, I know his intentions are not kind, for the night has taken over his soul, and it's like I'm seeing a reflection of my siren self when it takes control of me. He blows flames from his fingertips, and this time they scorch the end of my dress and travel upwards. He steps towards me, sending more flames in my direction, a wall of heat, pain, and death.

I leap into the water, and then I am yanked down, down, down, pulled by some invisible force. I kick my legs. "No!" I want to yell, but the light is fading, and I do not know where the water is taking me.

Water is my friend, but I also need air, and for whatever reason, my siren self isn't kicking in. It's as if a part of me has momentarily vanished. I swim toward a tree trunk, kicking my legs hard, and pressing my hand to its rough bark, not even sure why. I wait and hope.

A moment later, I feel that my lungs no longer ache, and when I open my mouth, I can breathe, but this isn't possible. There isn't any air under the water. Then, I see that I am inside a giant tree trunk, and that there is air coming in through the opening at the top of the tree.

I sink down upon a chair made of wood, and gaze around me, feeling sure I am a guest in someone else's home, but who lives here, and who rescued me?

"So many questions, child," a booming voice says, "And not many answers."

I look around the room, shocked to hear something or someone speaking to me. Water drips down my legs and trickles from my long hair.

"Who's there?" I call out, putting my hand instinctively to my sword.

"It is the master of this house. It is I, the living tree," says the voice.

"Did you bring me here?" I ask.

"I don't have the power," says the voice, "The water flows where it wills."

"Why am I here?" I ask.

"I cannot answer that," laughs the tree, and its inner trunk jiggles and shakes, "Why would the water have brought a siren to me?"

"Can you tell me anything? I am lost," I say.

"As are we all in this world," says the tree, "All I can say is this. Go back to the skeleton, and together, break the curse, else the darkness overtakes us all."

"I don't have what it takes to break the curse," I say, "Why is it my concern?"

"Love is just like a plant. It grows over time, if you tend to it," says the tree.

"I don't want this road," I say.

"No one said you did, now did they?" laughs the tree again, "No one ever asked me if I wished to grow. And no one asked me if I wished to be a tree either."

I don't see what's so funny. Had my brother lived, life would have been good. He knew how to stand up to my mother. Her voice did not affect him, not in the way it affected everyone else. He would have protected me from this. He was, in many ways, like the skeletons.

I thought I would hate Skully. I thought I would despise him if he ever attacked me, yet I do not. It was not Skully, but some other beast inside of him who did the attack. And there was something else in his eyes, something besides hatred. There was confusion and darkness. And now I only feel sorrow so deep I cannot explain it, just like I feel sorrow when I think of my mother and her voice, and the side of myself I hate.

I lift up my chin, stand tall, and take a deep breath of the sweet air. I wish that there was someone to tell me what I ought to do. How I ought to live, but since there is no one, I must choose, and it seems there is only one choice before me. Insane as it is, I will go back to Skully. To break the curse, for what else is there left to hope for? I cannot return home, not now. At least if there is peace, there is hope for life.

"Very well, bring me back to Skully," I say, but when I look up through the tree's center, I see that it is still night. Far off in the distance the stars still shine like beacons in the night.

"First we rest," says the tree, and soon a soft snoring sound of leaves, bees and winds begins. I am lulled to sleep, and when I wake, I am refreshed and the fears of the night are but a fuzzy memory.

I stretch and stand at the tree's center. With a laugh, the tree sends me upwards, as if a giant gust of wind is beneath me, and I float upwards and out, falling up into the water with a splash. When I resurface, the sun is shining and I see that our raft is still here. Skully is upon our raft, and he smiles when he sees me. He holds out his hand, and I take it, allowing him to pull me back onto our raft.

Chapter Five - Water's End

♥

"You tried to burn me up last night," I say, throwing a block of water at him. He shrieks and jumps as the water splashes over his bones.

"You didn't need to go do that, now did ye?" he says, "I hate the feel of water on me bones."

"Are you a pirate or aren't you?" I ask, shaking my head, and keeping a lookout for islands. I don't want to be at the mercy of Skully's flames tonight.

I keep on thinking about the tree's words. I wonder what the secret is to break the curse. I keep on wondering about love, and what it is. *Can something I've always thought was a terrible burden be something truly beautiful?*

"We are coming to a place where the water ends," Skully says.

I see what he means, for ahead of us is land, stretching as far as I can see, but it looks like a land that is dark and foreboding.

"Is that the place where the knights won't go?" I ask.

"Aye" Skully says, "And there be treasure there also, and after that, the place we seek."

"What does the treasure matter?" I ask. "Treasure will not keep us safe."

"It may matter," Skully says, "One never knows."

"All I need and want right now is a good bowl of food and a bed to sleep in, without wondering if I'm going to be burned up by my guide," I grumble and look at the dark lands looming ahead with a touch of sorrow. I don't wish to leave these waters that feel like a blanket of protection, and yet, I know the Knights are powerful, and I cannot risk them finding me.

Why I'm trusting a skeleton makes no sense to me, yet the water seems to whisper that it will be all right, and it nudges our raft towards shore, almost lifting us right onto the sand, as if we are no longer captains of this boat.

We are pitched onto the beach and I tumble after Skully, getting a face full of sand. I feel the grit between my teeth with my tongue. Skully just stands up and stretches his arm bones out. The Wood looms beyond, dark even in the daylight.

Chapter Six -
Curses

♥

"Let us go," Skully says.

I walk into the Wood. I glance back and glimpse the Knights on their boats in the water, as they turn around and head back toward the safety of their homes, and my heart longs to go with them. To once again be a part of my old, comfortable world.

Skeletons of varying shapes, sizes, and colors approach Skully, but they don't look happy to see him.

"Here be a dirty human-loving skeleton!" laughs a skeleton whose bones are a purplish hue, and whose hair hangs down in long dreadlocks.

"Aye," say the others, "Shall we hang him up to dry? Let's have our fun with him first."

"He has fire," says one.

"We can take it," says another, "No problemo."

"Huzzah!" they say in unison.

They advance upon him, using not only their bows and arrows, but their natural giftings. I see smoke, and I see blood, and I feel their evil powers flowing toward Skully. I run toward the shore and grasp two blocks of water. I hurry back to the mob and I hurl the water toward the skeletons, but it only falls down upon their heads, and they laugh it off.

"The silly girl thinks she can use water to overcome us?" One of the skeletons grabs me and pulls my hands behind my back so that I cannot move, much as I kick and struggle, and even as I send my heart out to the water, it does not come. This island must be an evil place indeed, if even the water will not aid me.

I turn to see them advance on Skully and push him down. They begin to take him apart piece by piece.

"Please!" I call, "I can show you where the treasure is."

"Treasure?" scoffs the leader, "And what use do we be having with treasure? We're half-dead. We don't need food, nor clothes, nor any-thing but arrows, and a will to fight."

"You can use it to break the curse. To buy love," I lie.

The skeletons gaze toward me with their blackened eye sockets, and a shine enters them. A greedy gleam.

"Take us to the treasure, and be quick-like," the leader says.

"First, we must find the map," I say.

"Aye," Skully says.

"Show us where the treasure is then," the lead skeleton says, "And we will spare his life and the life of you, human scum though you be."

I step forward, hoping there is actually such a treasure, and that if there isn't, we may escape before they find out they've been duped.

We walk into the forest, being pushed from behind by our captors. I glance over at Skully, hoping he will give me a hint where to go, yet at least these creatures are not wise enough to sense my lie, not yet.

Skully walks on ahead, and as we proceed deeper into the dark forest, I feel a suffocating presence. *Are these trees friendly?* A deep hush is in the forest. Not a bird sings its song, and not a butterfly passes by.

The skeletons complain and push each other back and forth. "We could be having ourselves a meal now," says one, eyeing me hungrily.

"What boss says goes," says another.

"Ye want the curse broken or no?" says a third.

I feel a shove from behind and I stumble over a stick in my path.

My stomach churns, and I feel that I might vomit. Skully isn't like that. He has protected my life. That is all I can think of to keep me sane. To keep me hoping. Hoping for something. Or someone. In goodness. Kindness. Even in this desolate place where humans are food.

The trees bend down toward us, but they do not comfort me like the great trees of the water. Their spirit seems one bent on evil. It's like when I stir up my tea and taste it, and it tastes bitter. It's like that in my chest. Except, here and there, there is sweetness, like the tree that took me in and saved my life. Every so often, there is a taste of honey, though bittersweet.

When the skeletons have tied Skully and me up and have gone on their nightly wanderings, I look over at Skully. *Is he there?* He strains against the ropes and bites at the air, his soul lost within the curse. I look away. I can't stand seeing him like that, but do I look any better when my siren-self consumes me? I shudder when I think of what I've done when my own cursed side takes over. The night stretches on, and creatures are heard screaming in the distance. Creepers explode.

When morning finally dawns, our captors return. At least I can stand up and stretch my legs, which have fallen asleep. They ache as the feeling returns, and we continue on, and the Skully of the day returns.

The skeletons are impatient, asking how much longer until we reach the treasure. I look over at Skully, and he nods and holds up his hand.

I look down and cannot believe that there is an X on the ground, faded, but still there. It can't be this simple. It can't be this easy. The skeletons start to dig, and they dig for most of the day, but there is nothing.

"If we don't find anything, it's the end for you and lover boy," says the leader with a smile and a tip of his pirate hat.

Finally, there is a clanking sound, like music to my ears. There is indeed a chest, and inside, there is treasure. Gold coins, enough to fund an army. Enough for me to regain my place in society. To be free of this place. I look wistfully at it for only a moment. I have no choice but to give them what I promised or forfeit my life.

"Let us go now," Skully says, "We gave you what ye wanted."

The leader says, "Untie them."

We are released, and the skeletons carry the treasure away, chuckling.

"How much time do we have before they find out you can't buy love?" I whisper.

Skully shrugs, "A few weeks maybe, but by then we'll be far from here."

When darkness begins to settle, we stop, but there's no water anywhere to be seen.

"What are we going to do?" I say.

"The trees might welcome you in," Skully says, "If ye treat them kind."

"So, what do I do?" I ask, feeling like a child being asked to spell my name for the first time.

"Don't ye know how to be a tree hugger?" Skully asks.

"No, it isn't proper," I say, but when was I in favor of being proper? Never. No, deep inside, I always hated proper, especially when politeness is so often a mask for evil.

I walk up to the closest tree, one that smells like honey, and wrap my arms around it, feeling ridiculous, but I'm too exhausted to focus on my embarrassment.

A moment later, there is a rumbling sound, and the heavenly smell of sweet pine rushes into my nostrils. A rustling sounds and the door creaks open at the tree's center. The door is barely tall enough for me to fit through. Skully gives me a push, and I stumble into the tree's center. It is homey, as if this place is made for guests, and all manner of birds flit through the tree and roost in its inner branches. There is a bed, and there is even water, flowing down the tree's trunk, and pooling in a bowl-like formation in the center of the room, as if this place was made for those like me. I long to put my feet into the water. To be refreshed, but I wait.

"Thank you," I whisper.

The trees are sacred. They are alive, and this one too, has welcomed me in. When the stars blink down at me through the top of the tree, and in this moment, I trust there is someone looking out for me. I stretch out upon a bed of leaves, and for the first time since I stepped foot on this island, I feel safe.

Chapter Seven - Training

❤

I am woken in the morning by a knocking sound. I stretch, and when I open the door, Skully stands in the doorway. "Can't you let a princess have her beauty rest?" I ask, wishing I could stay in this tree forever.

"Ye still care about that?" Skully says.

"Yes," I say, "I mean no, it's just...I don't want to leave."

I'll do as you ask. My promise to my brother runs through my mind. A promise I am nowhere near keeping. Even if I regain the throne, will the people accept me as their Queen? Now that I am far from the castle, the life I once knew is quickly fading. I am in a world where power, money, and all worldly things no longer matter.

"Practice time," Skully says, tossing me a bow and arrow. I catch the bow in my left hand. "You'll need a whole lot more than a beautiful voice in these woods."

We take turns shooting at a stone. His aim is always better than mine. I continue to miss, again and again.

Skully says I need to rest, but I keep on shooting until my fingers ache, my head thrums, and my stomach growls.

Finally, Skully tackles me to the ground, forcing me to stop. I resist, trying to rise again, but Skully is stronger. I lie back, with a laugh, surprised that I am not afraid. I look up at the trees, their canopy of green making me stop in wonder, and the smell of sweet green grass fills my nose. I should be afraid, but I'm not, and I don't understand how this can be, with a skeleton pinning me to the ground. He grins and rests back on his heels. I get up and sit down to eat. *Is this what it feels like to be free? To be my own woman?* Skully sits by me as I chew. Immediately, I am refreshed. I continue to practice, and when my arrow zings into the tree, Skully lets out a whoop of joy.

I can't help but smile at his excitement. Here I am, shooting arrows in the middle of the Wood. It feels like a dream come true. To be far from the castle and all of its rules. Not wondering what others will think of me. Not dreading what my mother will have me do.

"Tell me, how do you protect yourself from the siren's call?" I ask the question that has been burning in my mind all day.

"I use me bones, of course," he says, with a twinkle in his eye.

"Your bones?" I ask, not understanding, and maybe not even believing how bones could protect one from a song so strong.

"Ye can do it too," he says, "If ye practice. Every bone has power over the flesh, but most don't use the power they have."

It sounds like some kind of strange magic. Like something that cannot be possible, and yet I've seen Skully's powers, and my mother has the same power in her veins.

"Teach me," I say, still feeling a little strange that a skeleton of the Wood could be my teacher and friend.

"For me it is natural to use me bones, yet for yer kind, who depends much on the flesh, it is a different matter," he says, looking down at the bones of his feet. He scratches his skull with his finger bone."It will take time."

"We don't have much time," I say. "How long until she, or her Knights, find me?"

Skully nods, and slaps his finger bones together. "Well then," he says, "Let's begin."

He touches a hand to my chest, and I feel the energy coming from him, coursing through me, like the sea and the wind and the trees.

"Feel that?" he asks, his eyes sparkling.

"Yes," I say, almost unable to speak. It is so strong, I want to hide from its beauty. It is wholly different than my mother's song. Like darkness is to light.

"That same power is in you," he says, "Is in all of us. You connect yer song to bones, and when you have done so, you be protected."

"Connect my song to my bones?" I ask, still not understanding, for I have always thought of a song as an outward thing. Something to be shared. Something to be used for magic.

"How does it work?" I ask, still tasting his power on my tongue, and desiring to have the same thing. Desiring the sweetness. The ability to be free.

"It is a dance," he says, taking my arm in his and twirling me round. The trees spin, and I feel that if we weren't being chased, I could stay here forever, till the end of time.

"We don't have time for this," I say, but Skully is as relaxed as if he were taking a bath in the castle, yet even the image of this in my mind makes me smile.

"There always be time for dancing," he says, spinning me faster. I can feel his bones vibrating along with mine, as if we are in harmony with one another. I want to pull away. I feel a song begin within me. A siren song flows from me, and yet it seems to come somewhere from within. From my ankle bones. From my clavicle and my rib cage. My bones are beginning to sing, but when Skully releases my hand, the singing stops as quickly as it began, and all is suddenly still.

"I lost it," I say, "I lost the connection." I look up at the forest canopy, and then at Skully.

"You had it, be for a moment," he says, clapping me on the back.

"Ow," I say, rubbing my shoulder.

He bows apologetically. The sky is darkening. I know that our training must be done for the day.

Chapter Eight - Creepers

♥

Morning dawns as silent as a lamb.

Out of nowhere, an arrow zings into the tree right next to my left ear. I duck down instinctively, and look around, wildly searching for our attackers.

"Run," Skully says.

I don't need to be told twice. I leap up and run after Skully, arrows flying in all directions. An explosion goes off ahead of us, and I really hope there aren't creepers in this part of the woods, but when I glimpse their green and black faces, I know we aren't so fortunate.

"Creepers," I hiss.

"Stay cool," Skully says. He begins to whistle a tune and does a dance.

"Join Skully," he says.

I do as he commands, my body screaming at me to run.

I follow Skully's quirky movements, and although I never was good at whistling, I manage to sing along, a little, feeling that this is not going to work. I wait for the creepers to explode. Blow me up. Die. I wait for the inevitable, but when I only hear laughter, I can't believe it. The creepers are just standing there laughing, and a moment later, they move backwards and go back to wherever they came from.

"Move quickly," Skully says, "More may come. And some of my kind be angry to see me with you."

It would be far worse if my kind found me with a skeleton, I think. We are two strangers living similar lives. *Does Skully know what I'm capable of? If so, why is he helping me?*

I step forward, with a new confidence, not in myself, but in this strange skeleton who just saved my life. I wish I was the one who could save his life for once, but here I am, playing the pathetic female princess, yet again. Since childhood, I vowed I would be tough. That I would be different from the princesses I read about in the fairy tales, but I never knew how to follow my dream. Maybe now is the time when my dreams will finally come true. When I can finally be the person I've longed to be.

We run through the Wood, Skully pulling me along, until we reach two doors hidden by crawling ivy. Skully reaches out with a skeleton key, turns it, and a brilliant light comes forth, drawing me into itself. A moment later, I'm standing in front of a shelf filled with books. I gasp. The room itself is not what is beautiful, but the books, with their shining spines and the lovely smells of aged paper and ink.

Chapter Nine - Hidden Library

♥

"How did you find this place?" I ask.

Skully just lifts his shoulder blade into the air. I suppose he won't be telling me his secret, not now.

"It is a place I've long known about," he says with an air of mystery. A glorious purple light is coming from a giant book at the center of the room, and I reach out to touch it, but Skully slaps my hand.

"Ow," I complain. "Don't touch," he snaps.

I carefully examine the books on the shelves, being sure to clench my hands behind my back.

"You might need to bind me," I say.

"Ye love books that much? " he laughs.

Skully walks to the center of the room, and speaks, but it isn't until I look closely do I see a tiny snail sitting on an enormous oak desk.

The snail gazes up at Skully, and blinks its large liquidy eyes.

"We be needing a book on.." Skully says in a whisper so faint, I don't catch the words.

The snail sneezes and his small red cap flies off of his head. With a shake of his gray head, the snail says, "This way, my optimists, this way. There's only one book about that."

We follow the snail at a painfully slow pace to the back corner of the library, where, collecting dust is a thin stack of books, which the snail points to with his large eyes.

"There," he says, "But don't say I didn't warn you. Opening those pages, even in this room, has consequences."

He makes his way, sliding back toward his desk. Skully and I look at each other, but I know he isn't leaving here without reading this book, consequences or not.

"Are you sure?" I ask, even though I know the answer already. "There be no turning back now," he says.

Skully picks up a book and opens it to the middle.

"Look at this page," Skully says, as we settle into some mossy green chairs, situated under two dim lamps. The book itself shines brighter than any of the lights in the library, almost so that we don't require a lamp.

The book tells the history of our world, and how the wars began.

A skeleton and a human loved one another, and yet there was an evil sorceress who, out of jealousy and hatred, cursed the skeletons, to forever be at war with humans until the end of time. There is one however who can break the curse, out of a great act of love, bringing peace to the world. When the love is brought into the light for all to see, then the curse will no longer have its power, and the Sorceress will fade, out of time and history. Yet, for anyone reading these words, there is a great risk. For with this knowledge, comes much danger and many dark foes. Beware to all who read this, and God-speed.

"Very well. Sounds simple enough," Skully says, closing the book with a snap. He doesn't put the book back on the shelf, but slips it into his rib-cage.

"Is that a good idea?" I ask.

"This book be our road-map to ending the curse," he says.

I sigh, and put my hands to my hips. "And what about this evil sorceress? And the warning at the end? Don't we have enough foes already?"

I glance up nervously at the ceiling, half expecting something to drop down and attack me at any moment.

"Love be for anyone who practices it, and with love comes many foes," he says, as if it were a simple thing.

"It doesn't say anything about what this one is to do," I say, still wanting everything to fit into a box, a list, or a schedule.

"It says everything, yet we don't understand," Skully says, stretching out his bone fingers and cracking them one by one. "We leave...at daylight. The curse has no power in these walls."

I yawn and stretch out on a sofa made of moss and autumn leaves. My eyes are closing, and the next thing I know, I'm being shaken awake.

I half expect to find Mary leaning over me with a warm plate of food, but I only smell old, beautiful books. I open my eyes and I see Skully's gray face, and the books behind him. I sit up with a gasp, my heart racing. Then, I remember. I'm still very far from home.

"Quick, we must go," he says, "They have come to the one place I said they'd never go."

He pulls me to the door, and we step out just as dawn reaches through the trees, like long fingers saying hello.

Chapter Ten - Secret Tunnels

♥

S kully carefully covers the doors with ivy, and we step onto the dewy ground.

The sound of footsteps are heard in the distance, and my heart sinks. I thought we were safe here. That the Knights wouldn't come, but there is a smell in the air that I know too well. It is the smell of the Knight's magic, like metal on my tongue. *Are they no longer afraid of this place? Or am I so valuable that they would risk anything to see me dead?*

"If we call upon the One, we might yet survive," Skully says.

"Can the One rescue us?" I ask.

"He can do anything, when it be time," Skully replies.

I hear their shouts of "This way, they went this way! Quickly!" We run, but they are fast. They are cunning. My kingdom has the best trackers. And, every Knight is trained in magic of every kind, even the magic to resist my voice, if they choose to use it, and why wouldn't they? They are trained in things most do not understand. They are trained by the Queen herself.

They are close now. I can feel them, and hear them, and I hope they cannot hear my ragged breaths, nor sense the fear in my chest. Even if the Sea comes, and even if my song is strong, they have magic to counteract every move I make. My body is rigid, and every step is that of fear, adrenaline, and ragged hope.

Skully pulls some vines from the forest floor, and there is a door. He pulls on a rope, and the door opens, revealing an underground tunnel. The Knights are right behind us, although they look different than I remember. They look so much stronger, as if they have gained extra powers.

If I don't go with them, the rumors will quickly spread that I am a traitor. If I go with the Knights willingly, my mother will still find a way to give me the appearance of evil. Either way, I face death in one form or another.

"Go," Skully says.

I stand on the edge, looking down into a black pit.

Next thing I know, I feel a push from behind and I'm flying down the tunnel hole, landing at the bottom, Skully flying right toward me from above.

I roll out of the way and find that the tunnel is not as spooky as I expected. Skully lands next to me with a clatter of bones. There are lights down here, lots of them, dotting along the ceiling like twinkling stars. It is beautiful. Like a storybook fairy tale tunnel.

"That wasn't a nice tumble," I say, rising and dusting myself off.

I sigh and step forward. My first thought is, *how many spiders live down here?* My second thought is, *this looks like an entrance to an underground civilization.*

"Is this where you live?" I ask.

Skully laughs, "A pirate knows no home."

"Then, who lives down here?" I say.

"Skully hopes we don't find out," he says.

I run to keep up, watching my step for any spiders that might appear, my heart beating fast. Every scuttle makes me reach for my sword, even though I am still as unskilled at sword-fighting as a one-year-old just learning to walk. I look around, searching for water of any kind. If there is water, there is hope for us both, but it is as dry down here as a desert. I cannot sense the far-off sea, and my water canteen is almost empty.

The path is straight, and despite the darkness, so far it's a lot easier than above ground. But just when my heartbeat is beginning to slow, I hear the sound of people singing, a most glorious sound, like merry bells and laughter and a little bit like light.

"Gnomes," Skully hisses, pulling me down to the floor, "Hide."

Gnomes? I've heard wonderful stories of gnomes, and it's always been my dream to meet them. Are they as wonderful and kind as in the stories? I peer over the stone that we are hiding behind, while Skully tugs at my sleeve. I have to see them. Just once, but I don't get the chance, for a moment later, something drops over us.

I tug at the ropes, but Skully only looks at me. We are trapped.

"Why are you just sitting there?" I say.

Skully just shakes his head and hisses, "Magic net."

"We have to try," I say. *Why does he just sit back on his pathetic bones and not do anything? If I just had my enchanting book, maybe I could escape. Maybe I could do something.*

I try singing, a strained song through my dry throat, a song that sings of ropes untangling, of prison bars breaking, but my voice feels weak, and I have no connection to my bones. I want to scream. My voice has not often failed me, but in these nets, it is weak. Next, I take out my sword and run the blade back and forth against the rope, until a shock travels up my arm and to my neck. I drop my sword and crumple into a ball, rocking back and forth until the pain subsides.

Skully is correct. This net is magical, and with the net comes some magical beings. The gnomes. They peer down at us past their large noses and long beards, and gaze down at us in wonder.

"A skeleton and a siren, what a wonder," says a gnome with a beautiful purple cap over the top of his fuzzy white hair.

"My lord, the prophecy," exclaims another with a red cap over gray hair.

"Let me kill that skeleton for stepping foot in here," growls a third, with a floppy orange cap over a silvery head of hair.

I sing a song of release, but I know they cannot hear me. The net is their protection as well as my prison.

One gnome steps into view with such an air of authority, and such ferocity, I am afraid of seeing this little gnome angry. He has the whitest hair, and it flows down to his ankles, and he holds in his hand a scepter of gold.

"They have a mission," he says, "And we must make sure that it does not come to pass. For if it does, the mobs and the players will be one, and we will fade into nothingness."

"Let the girl go free," Skully growls, "And keep me."

The gnome only says, "We need her."

"I go wherever she be," says Skully.

"Take care of this nuisance," says the gnome with the white hair.

With that, the gnomes begin to disassemble Skully, bone for bone. First, taking off the skull and placing it beside me, then the finger bones, arm bones, the foot bones, the leg bones, and the ribcage. All of it is thrown into a pile as if he were nothing more than trash.

But he's not trash. He's alive. He *has* to be alive. I don't know why I'm crying. I don't understand what's going on.

The gnomes walk away, leaving me and this pile of bones alone. I close my eyes and wish I could pretend this wasn't happening. Wish I could put him back together.

"Skully," I whisper, but I get no answer. This is ridiculous. I'm talking to a pile of bones, but it doesn't feel ridiculous to me.

I sing his name, again and again, as if doing so will bring him back to life.

People can't be put back together, yet I've seen Skully put himself back together many times. I pick up the small bones of his feet, trying to remember their order. Then, I place the leg bones on top of the foot bones, then the hip bone, then the bones of the spine, and the rib cage. Each bone nudges me on, as if it too wants to be put back together, but just when I am almost finished, the skeleton collapses, and the bones scatter across the tunnel floor.

I put my head in my hands. *What am I missing?* I scoop Skully's Skull up into my arms, as if he will speak to me.

I pull at the cords of the net, helpless and trapped. I move my foot, and one of the bones is shoved through the net and onto the floor outside. The bones start to dance around on the floor, jiggling and wiggling about. I quickly push as many bones through the net as I can, and watch as they all start to dance. I am a little frightened, but more than this, strangely curious.

The bones dance around the net in a whirlwind so fast that the strings of the magical net begin to pull apart. I crawl through the opening and into the whirling bones, the wind whipping through my hair. Someone is calling my name. I open my eyes.

I crawl through the wind that pushes against my ears, my face, my chest, and my body.

"It's me," I say.

The whirlwind stops and listens to my voice. The bones hover by my head, as if waiting for me. I should find this creepy. I should run, but instead I'm singing to these bones again. I'm singing to Skully. My bones are singing to his bones.

"Come together, come back together now," I sing.

A toe bone nudges me, as if it wants me to pick it up. I do. The bone nudges my hand and I put it in place on the ground. Another bone hops into my hand, and I place it next to the other bone, one by one.

When the toe bones are arranged, then the ankle bone, the leg bones, the hip bones, the spine, and the arm bones, and finally the skull, I hear a familiar voice. I turn to see him, and it still doesn't seem possible. It must be a dream, but if it is a dream, I want to believe it.

"What happened?" Skully asks.

"Doesn't matter, let's run," I say, and I take Skully's hand and lead him the way I thought we came, yet I soon find out that it isn't the way we came at all, not even close.

Right now, I have a terrible craving for some of Cook's cheese and broccoli soup, and a glass of milk, which of course I cannot have, and my tender princess feet are not used to running across hard surfaces, and everything is starting to hurt from the bottom of my smooth feet to my temples.

"So, if someone tears me apart, can I be put back together too?" I ask.

Skully nods his bald skull as we crawl into a smaller tunnel and start to squeeze through.

"There is One who can fix every part of us," Skully says.

"Just like there's a magician who can make water into milk?" I say, his words sounding ridiculous to me.

"Few trust anymore," Skully says in a low whisper, "But there is One."

I wish I could believe this. I wish for somebody who can take all of the brokenness and make it new. It sounds too good to be true. Too wonderful. Too much like the fairy tales I stopped believing in long ago. If fairy tales were true, I would have found my prince, and I wouldn't be controlled by my mother's voice.

"And the One will come and put us together?" I ask.

Skully nods, and we reach a point in the tunnel where we can both stand, but the light is not growing stronger, but weaker, and I know I've made a terrible mistake.

"We're going deeper into this pit, not the other way around," I say.

"Aye," Skully says, "We must go deeper into the darkness to reach the light. And once we are in the light, we will follow the map on our journey."

Skully views everything in an upside-down way.

"I would rather not face the darkness," I sing quietly, my song comforting me.

"Aye," he says.

"Did you hear that?" I ask, my heart beating fast.

Something red flashes in front of my vision. Several red dots, and a dark body. My stomach wrenches at the stench of rotting meat.

Chapter Eleven – Web

♥

"Spiders," Skully hisses, and he runs on ahead, while I struggle to keep up, peering through the darkness to see what's in front of my own feet, and straining to hear any new sounds.

We don't make it far before we reach an impasse. Spider webs as thick as my wrist are crisscrossed across the path. I take out my sword, hacking at the webs, yet shocked when my sword only comes swinging back up toward my face, the web intact. We are trapped on both sides, and the spiders sit on their haunches, laughing at us, clicking their jaws, and preparing to feast on us.

"Where is that one that you spoke of now?" I ask.

"Always near," says Skully, and he does not look afraid. He stands tall and looks the spiders in the eye.

"Leave us," Skully says, as if he were talking to a naughty pet. The spiders scratch and claw and hiss at Skully's words. "Leave us NOW!" Skully says, his voice taking on a commanding tone. I wait and watch, but the spiders are not listening to Skully. They only laugh.

"You are only a skeleton. You are not the One, and she is but a water Princess."

"Yet the One is here, with me," says Skully, stepping forward, his body taking on a lighter glow, as if a fire were lit within his bones.

"Dinner Time!" the spiders laugh, ignoring Skully.

The spiders rush forward. Skully steps in front of me, his bow and arrow held at the ready. He lets an arrow fly, but it only bounces back towards him.

I sing, "Leave us now! Leave us now!" but the spiders must have a magic that protects them. They too have something that doesn't allow my song to penetrate their flesh. They laugh and prepare to feast on us.

I remember something from a story my mother used to read to me. I reach into my pocket, searching until I find its small, round shape. I take out my mirror, pointing it toward the spider that is facing Skully. The spider screams out when it looks down and turns to run down the passageway. I hold the mirror out in the other direction, and this spider, too, scuttles off and away, letting out a great wail.

I sit down, and Skully sits beside me, stretching his long leg bones out and humming a tune. I am glad the spiders have gone, at least for now. The only trouble is, we're still inside their web.

"Can you do the whirlwind trick again and get us out of here?" I ask.

Skully shakes his head. "Skully cannot, for it wasn't Skully. Skully asks the One to come, yet the One comes when it is time."

"Well, it seems to me it's about time," I say, crossing my arms over my belly, shivering.

The tunnels are cold and damp. The walls go drip, drip, drip. Water droplets drip down onto the back of my neck. I keep my mirror on my lap and try to keep my eyes open. I'm just so tired and there is a deep darkness here.

"Skully watch. Princess sleep," Skully says.

I want to protest, but I know that if I don't sleep, I won't have the strength to escape. I close my eyes, the images of giant spiders flitting through my mind, yet however unrelaxed I may be, somehow sleep takes me. I snap awake to Skully shaking me by the shoulders.

My body immediately tenses, my stomach tightens. The cave is dark, but I can just make out a shape in the distance. A bumbling rumbling sound, and a laugh, and soon a large finger reaches through the web, and plucks me out, dropping me into the tunnel. Then, the fingers return, doing the same for Skully, so that we are both out in the tunnel again. Free from the web. Free.

"Thank you!" I call, but all I see is the arm retreating through the top of the tunnel wall, and a whistling and great rumbling can be heard over our heads.

"Lovely," Skully chirps, "Lovely old giants."

"Why did he free us?" I ask.

"Can't someone do something nice without you asking why every time?" Skully sighs. "Some be kind, and some cruel. That is the way of it, Princess."

"I know this, it's just odd, that's all," I say.

"Well, the One has odd ways of getting things done. Don't try to understand. Just be glad," Skully nods.

"Agreed," I say, walking on. A light shines in my eyes, and the scent of pine reaches my nose.

I pick up the pace, running for the entrance. I run with everything in me, while Skully seems to glide along effortlessly. "Race you to the entrance!" I shout, as I run, and Skully leaps ahead of me, as quick as a deer. Something in me spurs me on, and I pass him, adrenaline and hope pushing me forward. Just when I reach the opening, I hear Skully hiss, and when I turn to look behind me, he is trapped. Great slimy arms wriggle all around him, crushing his bones, and taking him down.

Chapter Twelve - A Light

♥

I stop. Freedom is so close. Yet, I turn toward the opening. I hesitate for only a moment, and then, before I can even think about what I'm doing, I rush back into the darkness.

I hack at the slimy arms with my sword. Not even a notch is made in its flesh. My sword is more like a stick against these tough arms that are covered in a type of armor I've never seen. Strong and impenetrable. A face with many wolf heads, ferocious and biting and cracking every bone in Skully's body.

"Run," Skully croaks.

I'm tired of running. I'm tired of fighting, yet I will not abandon Skully. Insane as that sounds to me now.

"If you're there, help me," I call out, but to whom I'm speaking, I really don't know. If the One exists, I need Him now.

A large cat bounds into the tunnel, taking the wolf-headed creature by surprise. The cat scratches the wolves many heads, until they howl and retreat back into the tunnels, dropping Skully to the tunnel floor like a broken toy. I rush forward, but not before the cat picks Skully up gently in its mouth, and carries him out of the cave.

"Stop!" I shout. The cat turns and gently places Skully upon the ground. I breathe in and out, relief flooding me.

Skully is so broken, many of his bones are shattered, and yet, there may be hope.

When I take the pieces and put them together, it is easier this time, like a puzzle I've learned once before. Skully stands and he smiles, placing his pirate hat upon his skull. He bows and turns around and laughs, and says, "Good as new."

"How do you keep doing that?" I ask. "Do skeletons have never-ending lives?"

"No," he shakes his head, "As long as hearts are left, I re-enter this world," he says, hanging his skull. "I only hold one more heart now."

"Oh," I say. I know what this means. He doesn't have much time left. Not in this place where so many dangers lurk around every corner.

We leave the tunnel and enter the beauty of the forest, and nothing has ever felt more refreshing. The water tastes clear and wonderful, and every flower is tasty, although I never thought anything could be as delicious as a castle meal.

I can look at Skully without fear, and somehow, although it still seems impossible, as a friend.

Someone is waiting for us. He has his arms open wide, and I know him. I've known him forever and a day. Since the beginning of time. And He knows me.

"Fair Eloise, princess of the castle beyond," He calls, "And fair Skully, Master of the Wood."

I bow, feeling that I would be better suited to hiding in a hole, but the person lifts my chin with such gentleness and authority, and says, "Your journey has just begun."

"I was hoping this was the end," I say.

"There is much to be done yet, and still the darkness grows," He says, looking into my soul. "You must overcome the darkness and find love."

"How?" I ask, "How can I?"

"That is not for me to say," says the being who is so much more than a man. "But take heart, for I will go with you, wherever you go."

Skully nods, suddenly looking taller and wiser in this place, and his bones have taken on a golden color, the gray fading, and his eyes filling with light that makes his eyes look almost human. And around his neck bones, the man puts a compass. And to me, he gives a crystal that shines light in every direction.

My legs are stronger. My body no longer aches, and I feel as if I can think clearly for the first time. All of the fear I had is gone, and I don't want these feelings to ever leave. I could stay here forever, and soak in whatever this being has and is.

"Farewell, children," He says, first bowing to me and then to Skully.

"When will we see you again?" I ask, already the ache in my chest is growing. I wish he could come with us. Comfort us. Guide us. Help me every step of the way. Then, everything would be alright.

"Soon," He says, and when He is gone, and the clearing is empty, I no longer remember quite what He looked like, only that He knew me, and He cares for me in a way no one else ever could or will, and at least this comforts me, even as my heart is heavy.

And so, Skully and I continue on. We walk by day, and seek shelter by night.

"We are lost. We must ask the trees for their guidance," Skully says. "For the book has confused me, and I do not know which way to go."

I gaze up at the large trees all around me, beautiful with their strong, smooth trunks and their leafy branches, and green moss that wraps itself around them.

"Halloo!" Skully calls, throwing a pebble upwards at the tree. A moment later, there is a creaking groan as the tree comes alive, moving and stretching its branched arms to the sky.

"Why does the Skeleton wake me?" the tree asks. "For help, fair tree-King," Skully says.

"Don't flatter me," the tree scolds, "Tell me what you want, quickly. There is an evil stink in the air."

"Yes, it must be destroyed," Skully says.

"Ha," the tree bellows in a booming laugh. "You think you can do it?"

"I have a siren girl," Skully says, "And I have love, if but a little, and the book."

The tree's face moves, and eyes I didn't know it had, open to reveal purple irises with flecks of golden yellow. The tree bends down to examine me, and I wish I could hide away from his penetrating stare, but instead, I stand still as a stone.

The tree sniffs, as if smelling me, and closes his eyes. "Very well," he says. "Since you have no evil in your scent, I'll show the way, but it won't be easy, even if your words are true."

The tree takes the book in his limbs and sniffs the pages gingerly. His eyes brighten, and he points us to the path.

Chapter Thirteen - New Path

♥

"Follow the path, but do not wander to the left or to the right," the tree warns us.

We set off down the path, and it sounds simple, but the path before us already looks dark and not the least bit frightening. Of course, this is to be expected. The book said we would have troubles.

As we walk, the icy chill wind pushes its fingertips through my cloak, so that much as I wrap the cloth tighter around me, I still feel bitterly cold.

"You'll need to start using a bit of magic," Skully announces, as he marches onward. "And remember your gift of water and voice."

"Is there magic for staying warm?" I shout.

"There's magic for everything, if you know how to find it," Skully replies.

I shiver, and although his words should be a comfort, all I want right now is to be back in my warm bed at the castle, with cozy blankets piled ten feet high.

I sing to myself, "Warm water come. Warm waters," but the water doesn't come, not right now, and my voice doesn't comfort me. The water is its own master. This is what my mother taught me. She said you cannot control the water any more than one can control a siren, yet she knew how to control me, and for most of my life, I could not escape her voice, no matter how much I tried.

"Put the song into your bones," Skully says. "And your flesh can no longer be cold."

I sing the song, and push it down toward my leg and arm bones. I concentrate and let the song travel through me, and the more I sing, the warmer I feel.

"I think it's working," I laugh.

"Very good," Skully says.

Skully doesn't seem affected by the cold, his bones impervious to many things the flesh is not.

We press on, but just as I am beginning to feel that I can manage the wind, the air becomes calm, and the heat presses in on us, as if we walked from winter into summer in a moment.

Now, not only am I cooking inside, but outside as well.

"OK, now I must sing a cooling song?" I ask.

Skully shakes his head. "Now, you must let me cool you, for bones are cooler than flesh.

He touches his hand to my arm, and I do not want him to. I do not want to face the fact that the more I get to know him, the more I don't wish to leave him. His bones work their magic, and I am cooled, but I know there is a price. Skully's bones fade in color, only the slightest, but enough for me to notice.

"Don't sacrifice yourself for me," I say.

"I will decide who I sacrifice myself for," he says.

"Maybe we should just go home. Forget the prophecy," I say.

"It is not just some prophecy. It is life and death," he says solemnly.

"Right," I say. "And how do I know the prophecy is true, and we're not on some dead-end road?" I am weary and tired of the road.

"We don't know. We simply trust," Skully says, and he turns and keeps walking. I hurry to keep up. "The One wouldn't have sent us if it wasn't important."

"Very well," I say.

I'm out here in the sweltering heat, chasing some hidden prophecy, and a love I have no idea how to find. I want to give up. Lie down and rest, but I force myself forward.

The path darkens as evening sets in. Skully is walking at a snail's pace when we stop to make shelter. He has lost his energy for today, just as when I use my siren song, the energy it takes to produce it fatigues me. We stop and rest, and I hope there will be no enemies on either side.

I kneel on the ground, which is now hard. It is obsidian, the greatest stone in all the kingdom.

I touch my fingers to the stone, hoping it will bring me some clarity and strength. I'd always heard of obsidian's great powers, and when I look over at Skully, I see that he has regained some of his strength again. These stones are powerful.

Chapter Fourteen - Beauty and Ashes

♥

Our strength comes just in time, for a moment later, a beautiful woman approaches us. She smiles, and I am at ease. I want to trust her. To believe she'll make everything alright again. That she'll fix this mess I'm in, but my guard is up.

"Say you don't love him," she says, "And I'll let you live." A great torrent of water appears and laps at my feet, but this is not water I summoned. It is something deep and of the dark waters.

"Love who?" I ask, even though I know she speaks of Skully. And I don't understand why it matters to her who I love. I step back, hating the feel of this water and its dark whisperings at my feet. Feeling disgusting, and knowing that I need to put my shield up. I need to protect myself. I need to sing.

She looks over at Skully. "The skeleton, of course," she hisses, through her blood red lips.

"I'll give you everything you desire. Your kingdom. Power. Wealth. Beauty. Anything you ask for will be yours, just say you don't love him," she says.

"And what about my people? What will happen to them? What will happen to Skully?" I ask, summoning up my song from within me, and trying with all my strength to link it to my bones.

"Don't concern yourself with them. Look at what you can have. That's all that matters now," she says, and when I think about it, I do want these things. *I want everything to go back to how it was. She's offering me a new life. A way out. An escape. But, what's the catch?*

I gaze at my protector. The one who has been with me. I look at this beautiful woman. The one offering me all I could ever desire, but I cannot bring myself to say what she wants. I cannot say I do not love him, and I cannot say that I do love him, for I do not know. I touch the obsidian again, and I stand up, and walk to Skully, and clasp hands with the cold of his boned hand.

A song begins, and my song is not strong enough, even as I work to bring my song forth, I drop Skully's hand as her song weaves itself around my heart.

"You don't love him anymore, You don't love him anymore," the song wraps itself tighter and tighter around me, and the water rises to my ankles and then to my waist and my chest.

I am beginning to forget him. I am beginning to forget everything, and it feels wonderful. The song feels like life. It feels so right and good. *Of course, I don't love him. Of course. Of course,* my flesh says. The world I know whirls around speeding by, as we are spun round and round, so fast I'm sure this is how I will die, but at least I will die happy.

But then, as if by instinct, I reach my hand down and touch the crystal around my neck. I rub it until the light shines so bright I close my eyes tight. I hear a scream, and the world stops spinning. I drop to the ground in a jolting fall, and the song is broken. The water recedes. I rub my eyes, as if waking from a dream.

When I look up, the woman is gone, and Skully lies not far from me. I inch myself toward him, everything aching. The ache reminds me of when I escaped from the castle. An ache so deep I want to lie down and sleep forever.

Will the woman return? And why do I know her face? So familiar and yet so foreign to me. I gaze down at Skully, who seems to be asleep, but I cannot tell, for how does a skeleton breathe? *Where is his pulse if he has no heart?* I do not know why I am with a skeleton of all beings, nor why I lie down beside him, and wait. My body is empty and worn. My soul feels like it has been pinched into a million pieces. I need to find the sea. The Sea that cares for me. The Sea that is a part of me. I want to cry, and yet I cannot. I want to ask why, and yet what good will it do? I want to run from this bony creature, and yet, where will I go?

Night passes, and when the next day dawns, Skully isn't beside me. *Where has he gone?* I get up and call for him, only because I know I need his help, not because I care for him in any way.

"Boo!" I hear the rattling voice say, and I jump. I turn around to find his gray skull peeking out from behind a tree.

I put my hands on my hips.

"That wasn't very nice," I say.

"I wasn't ever very good at nice," he says, sauntering over to me as if he owns these very woods. He's a cocky little fellow.

"Who was that woman?" I ask.

"Don't you know?" Skully says, "She is the most powerful siren that ever lived."

I know who this is, and yet I don't wish it to be so. I know the woman I saw last night. It's all coming together now. *The voice, but what did she convince me of now? She is my mother, and I didn't recognize her.*

I've known this all along, and yet the truth hurts. It is too painful to bear. I do not want the woman to be her. I wish she were someone different. Anyone. And I am afraid of what she sang to me. The dark serenade she must have wound round my heart. I am always afraid when I cannot remember, for that is when I know she does her dirtiest work.

"What did she say to me?" I ask, my heart catching in my throat.

Skully just shakes his skull from side to side, "It was siren speech. I couldn't understand it. That is another way we remain outside of her control, and why she be hatin' us so."

I throw my boot down upon the ground in frustration. If I knew what she said, maybe I could avoid her control. Maybe I could sing it away.

"What have I done?" I ask. "Why can't she just let me go?"

"Ye have chosen love, " Skully says, "And that frightens her. For it be love and this book that will break the curse, and leave her powerless.

Frightens her? How can anything frighten her? She is powerful and unbeatable as the sea. Even my voice is weak in comparison to hers.

"I think you're talking about someone else," I say. "I haven't chosen love."

We walk together through the Wood, and everything feels wrong inside me. There are no mobs in sight, and there is a twinkling of the green leaves overhead, yet the day could be as dark as death. The birds have begun to sing, and when Skully reaches for my hand, I feel something breaking inside of me. Like all of the pieces that were broken have now shattered into even smaller pieces, and I too feel like I am nothing more than bones.

I pull my hand back and snap, "Don't touch me."

"We must find her and destroy her," Skully says. "Else she will destroy us both, and all of my people besides. She has waited forever to do so."

I shake my head. "No, I cannot," I say. He doesn't know what he is asking. *How can I destroy my own mother? It is not my task. Let someone else do it. Anyone else but me.*

"You cannot allow her to choose her time of attack. You must take her off guard," Skully says.

"You're not deciding what I will do or not do," I snap. "I never asked for this path. I won't do it. You cannot ask me to attack my own."

I stomp away through the damp leaves, ready to give up this quest. Tears threaten to push out of my eyes. I am not well, and I have treated my friend badly. Ready to give up on everything, but Skully is close behind. I know he won't let me out of his sight. I wish to be left alone. *Why is he with me? Why does he care for me when I despise his kind?*

"Eloise," I hear him say, but I don't listen. It doesn't matter what he says. He is a skeleton, and I am a siren. My mother is right. We can never be together, not if I wish to be successful. Not if I wish to live. *I should never have come here.*

There is a pop and a rush of air. I've heard that sound before. My heart sinks. I whirl around to face him, but when I look at the path I have taken, he isn't there.

"Skully?" I call out, panic spreading through my chest. What if she came back and took him captive while I was throwing a temper tantrum? I put my head in my hands, but I cannot let myself fall into self-pity now.

"Skully!" I call out again, but he isn't anywhere to be found. He has disappeared. I call out to the water. It comes, but it cannot save me. It does not answer me as to where my friend has gone. I call upon the seashells, hoping they will speak, and they only speak in a watery moan, and I know that all is not well with this skeleton. Somehow, I know he was my friend, even if I hate him.

I bury my head in my hands. I know where he has gone. She's taken him, and who knows what she'll do to him now? At first, I thought that I did not care. That I shall leave him to his fate and find my own path. I am sure that I hate him, and yet something else says that I do not hate him. Something or someone else whispers of another way, and when I stroke the light around my neck, I feel differently. I feel as if I am slowly waking from a dream.

"Finally," booms a tree overhead. "You have come to your senses now."

I gaze up at the speckled, green-eyed giant of a tree. I nod, and as he laughs, sending leaves down upon my hair, I know that now is no time for rejoicing.

"Take me to him," I say to the Seas. I float upon the water as it whips up and rushes forward, back toward home; the one place I do not wish to go, yet that is where he is, and that is the direction the book was taking us all along, much as I wanted to believe it was not. Much as I wanted to ignore what my bones were telling me.

I'm near the castle, and I hear her voice even before we reach the doors. Her voice is in my mind, just as my mother's voice always was. The dreaded sting. I no longer know whom I can trust. I no longer know who I am. I let the waters of the earth rise and touch the backs of my hands, comforting me a little. I prepare myself, inexperienced as I am. I sing a song of protection and store it in my bones, even though I will be weaker, it is better to be prepared.

When I reach the castle doors, memories flood my veins. Some of them wonderful, some dreadful, and some bittersweet. Once, I would have longed to return home, to those I thought cared for me. Once, I would have looked forward to their greetings, but now I only feel a sickening. A knowing that inside these walls, there is a voice that can control anyone it chooses, and this frightens me more than anything.

I pray to the waters for strength, and I search for the One, but he doesn't appear, at least not in physical form.

Chapter Fifteen - Taken

♥

"**I**f you want your lover, you'll need to come with me," I hear her say, her song melodic and beautiful. She speaks into my mind, yet I do not see her face.

"Will you promise me no harm?" I sing.

The voice doesn't answer. Of course, my mother will make no such promises. I step forward, and the waters tighten their grip on me, pulling me back a little with a strong pull of the current.

"I must go inside," I tell the Sea, even as it resists. I push my song from my bones and let it travel toward her, but she blocks it, as quickly as I expected she would. *Will I be able to protect myself from her attacks?*

I bring the waters with me, to the castle doors, and they pool around me, and sing *hush, hush.* There, my mother stands, in all of her glorious power, her guards materializing on every side of me. There is no escape now.

My mother does not need any chains to bind me. She begins to sing, and I am already weak, like a child once again. Even as I soothe my song through my bones, it only blocks part of her song, not all of it.

"Don't do this, mother," I plead, as her song begins.

I look over, and there is Skully, but he is in chains. What else can I expect? If I don't do as I'm told, then I will suffer for it. Just like the time I didn't wear my long proper skirt. I had to sit the entire day, and didn't get to go to the party. Except this is no mere party. This is life and death.

"Mother, be reasonable," I sing. "Do not let me die over our differences. Let me live!"

Skully smiles, and his eye sockets twinkle with a periwinkle blue. *How can he smile at a time like this? Does he know something I do not?*

My mother doesn't seem to hear me. She waves me away with her hand, and not even her eyes show any pity. Her teeth are sharp. Her lips are red, and she is as beautiful and as dangerous as she ever was.

"You cannot love," she laughs, "Nor can anyone truly love you. To die for false love is so pathetic, I could laugh, but that is what you have chosen, daughter."

I want to scream at her. So loud and so long. I want to sing a song of sorrow that reaches everyone's ears, so that everyone knows. I begin to sing, "I can love, I can love, I can love," but her song is more powerful and cuts my soul like ice, and soon I can no longer sing anymore, her song choking out my own. I only gasp, and my energy is spent. The guards take me to the dungeon, and I do not try to escape.

I look over at where I imagine Skully to be. Did they put him in the cell next to mine? I put my hand upon the cold wall, wishing I could speak to him, or see his face, one last time.

What did I think I would do? Just walk in, take over, and live happily ever after? Or that some great knight would arrive and rescue me? Why did I come here? I reach for the water droplet that stayed in my pocket and sing it a little song.

"What do you do when you're in a cage and there's no way out?"

"You swim," the droplet seems to say, for water has always spoken to me. It has a way of rippling and singing in its language, a language only the siren can hear.

I wish it were that easy. If only I could swim out of these bars and back out into the ocean, then I'd be safe forever. I could stay there, and live alone, deep beneath the waters, where no skeletons and none of my people live, not even my mother.

Do I summon the water now? Can it even hear me in these walls? I call out to the water, but it does not answer this call. It does not come.

"There is darker magic in these walls," says the squeaky water droplet. "Your song will not do good here."

"Of course," I sigh. *Is there a way for me to face my mother? A way to use my song to defend myself? A way out of this cell?* When I crumple to the floor, there is no comfort in my mind, only doubts and fear. *Am I going to die here?*

I call to the water in the castle, but it is dark and foreboding. There is no life here now. No living water full of light. I spend the night tossing and turning and fearing.

The next day, I am brought out of the dungeon and led to a high place before all the people. I see them, their faces blurred, and meshing together into a great black sea of faces. I want to hide my face in a hole and return to the wood, where at least I felt that someone cared for me. Here, where lies overcome the truth, there is little hope, but when I look up at the rain clouds, I wonder if they will listen to my call, and if they are kind floodwaters. A flood is just what I need.

"We were coming to take the Princess peacefully back to the castle, but she refused to come with us. She attacked us, as if we were the mob," the Queen's voice booms across the courtyard.

You are the mob, I want to scream the words out, but my mouth is gagged, and there is nothing I can say, not that it would matter. The rag tastes like damp dirt and pain. *You are the liar.*

"She makes friends with skeletons, embracing evil," she continues.

"Kill her! Kill her! Kill her!" the chanting begins. They cannot see me as anything but evil now. I have broken the rules, and now the Queen is making sure I pay the price. So, maybe she will win after all. If only I knew what we had read in the book. I think back to the words on the pages, a blur now. A distant memory.

I look for Skully, but I do not see him anywhere. I look for a friendly face, but there is none.

I can see the bright orange blocks below the gallows. There is no escape, and there is no chance for rejuvenation. No potion or golden apple or hidden magic can save me now. Not even a million ice cubes. And even if I had a potion, it would not last forever. No. No. No. This can't be happening, but it is. I have one thought now: *Was it Mother who was jealous? Was she the one in the story who did not find her true love? Is she the one who cursed the skeletons and sirens forever?*

I push against the ropes, wishing for some magic to save me, but the ropes remain firm. *Will Skully remember me?* I look out at the crowd of jeering people. People who once loved my father. Yet, how easily they turned against me.

"Now I'll give her a choice. If she chooses to have the skeletons destroyed, I will let her go free. If she does not, she dies!" roars the Queen, her boots clicking across the platform.

"Do I destroy the skeletons?" she asks, her icy gaze piercing my own, and even as her beautiful lips part, she knows my answer. Her smile says she has the victory.

She steps close to me, her perfect purple robe billows out behind her, auburn hair cascading down to her shoulders, and teeth as white and as sharp as a wolf's. She yanks the gag from my mouth, and I breathe in the air tinged with the smells of sweat, chaos, and anger.

Life stands before me, like a glowing, beautiful thing. *I can live.* All I have to do is allow the mobs to die. But Skully will die too. I know I do not love him. That I cannot love him, and yet I cannot let him die, and I don't know why. Maybe I'll never understand.

I spit the word out, in defiance of this place and all of its pious rules. And yet there is something else there, too. There is a tinge of the one thing that I said I would never have. There is *love*, somewhere beneath my siren veins.

"No," I spit out the one word that seals my fate, and she smiles.

But just as quickly, I begin to sing a rain song, calling the water to me, calling and singing from every bone in my body, I sing, and my mother's song rises up, clashing with my own. The storm clouds come. The rain falls, in great thick torrents, but my hands are still bound. I can no longer see in front of me.

There is a push from behind, as I am pushed toward the fiery lava burning underneath the platform. *This is how I am going to die.*

I fall through rain and think of Skully. Think of love, and think of the Sea. Someone catches me, hard bones colliding with my soft flesh. My body is swung upwards, and the ground rushes underneath my feet like a blanket that I clutch to, the dirt cool and welcoming. I force myself up onto my feet, dizzy. I hear a great commotion as the skeletons flood onto the lawn. Creepers also come, exploding and taking out the guards. I grin at my rescuer, through the oncoming rain.

"How?" I ask, but he waves my question away, as if it doesn't matter.

"Go," Skully motions for my mother, but I only feel sick inside. *How can I face her?* I shake my head and sink to my knees. There has to be another way. But, maybe I was meant to face her after all. Maybe there is no other way to break the curse.

"Is this where the book brought us?" I ask.

Skully nods. "The Queen only quickened our arrival here. She wants the book, more than anything else, so she may destroy it."

"Does she have it now?" I ask.

Skully smiles, and I know that he has more than one trick up his arm-bone.

I turn to see the Queen flee for the safety of the castle doors, and I follow, running after her, making sure to grab a sword on my way and a song, and even though my legs are still wobbly, and my body and mind resists, I press forward.

I call out to the Sea, and it comes, with an explosion and rushing of waves crashing toward the castle, and then it stops suddenly. It lulls at my feet, and surrounds me, like a pillar of water about me, as if to strengthen and fortify me. *Now, I am ready.*

Chapter Sixteen - Siren Battle

♥

She is waiting for me, and has the three-headed Wither at her side. I did not expect I'd fight her on my own. She knew I would come, just as mothers know many things about their children, that we do not know about ourselves.

I walk up the long aisle that is clothed in red, like blood. The same aisle I expected my brother to walk down. The same aisle all princesses and princes one day take on their way to becoming a king or a queen, but now? I am only walking toward death, for how can I overcome not only the Queen, but the Wither as well? I want to call out to Skully. Ask him to rescue me, but this is my battle, much as I detest it. Much as I hate what I am about to do.

"Naïve as ever," she laughs. "Do you really think you can win? We are alike you and I. Both sirens. Both devourers of life. "

No, I am not like her. I will not accept this as my fate. I will not be a devour-er. I will be a Siren who uses her powers for good.

"Was anything real?" I ask. "Did you ever love me?"

"I cannot love. None of us can. Any siren who believes they can love is a fool," she laughs, and calls her own Sea servants to her. I see that not only does she have the Wither, she has water on her side as well, and her waves are more tumultuous than mine have ever been, and her water has teeth and claws as sharp as a knife.

"What about mercy? Can you not at least have mercy on your own daughter?" I ask, the water swishing around my ankles gives me the strength to speak, and the words flow easily, like a song.

She smiles with her blood-red lips, and a chill envelops me instantly, taking the courage from me. I feel at once weakened and like that child I once was, all over again. I summon my song, letting it rush through my bones, washing away some of the chill, but not all of it.

"How can one have mercy on a skeleton-lover?" she asks. "You have joined evil. You have ignored all I ever taught you. You are no daughter of mine." She turns from me, and yet the Wither watches, and waits, ready to destroy me in an instant, and the water bites at me, and barks, wanting my blood.

"They aren't who you think," I sing, stepping forward, begging for her to understand. "They can be kind. They can be good!"

But when her teeth sharpen and her eyes turn a beautiful blue, I know that she won't listen to me. She has blocked my song forever. She has chosen her path. I have seen her look like this once before, and I had forgotten until now. This is the look of a Siren right before it eats. This is the look that I vowed I would never see on my mother's face again.

"Trusting them only leads to destruction," she says, coming toward me, as if to embrace me.

I stumble backward, singing, "Don't do this, Let me go, just let me go, and love me."

My mother swims toward me, her mouth warping into a giant mouth with sharp shark's teeth. My song wraps itself 'round my bones, and she cannot get close. She screams in frustration, her eyes brewing a dark green. Never before have I been able to stop her from evil, and now she is furious.

With one nod of her elegant head, the Wither comes down. A great storm bent on killing everything in its path, hurling explosive skulls right at me. I dodge them, just barely.

At the same time, my Mother's water rushes toward me, pulling me into its current and pulling me down with its icy grasp. I lurch for the healing water that obeys me, waiting for its warmth, willing it to come to my aid. I can feel the tug and pull as my water battles hers. As the warmth of the kind waters press and groan against the waters my mother wields.

I beat my fists and struggle for air. There is no air in this cold water. There is nothing here but death. I sing a small song, and begin to feel a seeping in of warmth. A little trickle against my wrist, then my other wrist, and then it travels to my lips, and I can breathe, if only a little, gasping air, sucking in and out.

I reach for more of my water. I reach for strength in song, and when I have gathered a little power, I hurl my water at the icy waters surrounding me. I make a small gap and slide through. I am free, momentarily, but I know that she is waiting for me, ready. This is how a Siren does things: weakening their prey, little by little.

When I reach the surface of the water, I take big gulps of air and look around me, searching for her. *Even if I find her, what will I do? How can I face her again when the cold water has taken most of my energy away?*

The Wither waits for me, a sloppy grin on his large face. But there is someone else here too, the Sea whispers. A friend, hiding in the shadows.

I step toward the Wither, and send my water upwards towards his face in a rush, blinding him. He staggers to the side, then roars, more angry than before. He reaches for me, and I run out of his grasp. I reach into my inventory for a pumpkin and some iron. I'm not fast enough. I am dragged upwards and into the storm itself, my body bending around and twirling in a sickening spin. I open my eyes, sand and dust blowing into them, blinding me.

Her laughter is all I hear, as I spin, and spin. And then I remember. A memory ever so small. A man turned to bones in moments. I was there.

As I spin, my mind spins, and there is only one face I see. Skully's face. The face of light in darkness. But even as I spin, I throw the pumpkin head on the iron, and an iron golem comes to life, fighting alongside me, until the Wither drops me back onto the ground.

I rise, shakily to my feet, and drink down a strength potion, given to me by the Sea-stars. I unsheathe my diamond sword, and as the golem attacks the Wither on one side, I come at the Wither from the other, whacking the Wither again and again, and again. It is stronger. It does not weaken, and what strength I had soon fades. Skulls fly through the air, coming one after another. I call out to my water. It is there, beside me, but it too is weak, and I can feel it gather around my feet, and travel up my arms and legs, coating my body in a slippery film. The skeletons arrive, coming by the dozens, their hard feet pounding along the ground, their hissing heard all through the castle. They fight alongside me, flinging arrows and swinging swords. I fling my water, and it comes down as rain, confusing the enemy and making it hard to see. The skeletons trample the Wither down into the earth, like ants swarming on a mound of rot, and the rain pummels the Wither into the earth, using every last bit of energy I have. Skully comes to my side, and I lean on him, too weak to even stand. I collapse onto a puddle, which soothes my aches and pains, and sings to me a lullaby. I float in water, and do not think of anything for a long time, but the Sea and the stars and Skully.

When I wake, I look around, but do not see my Mother anywhere, but I know she isn't dead. Sirens can sense other sirens of the Sea. Besides this, she would have found a way to stay alive, this I do know, but I cannot go after her now, and maybe I will never see her again. That is my hope, but it is foolish. *She won't rest until the skeletons are destroyed.*

Chapter Seventeen - Crowns and Crosses

♥

That evening, Skully picks up the crown and holds it out to me, but I shake my head, tell him it isn't time.

"We cannot crown her until the Queen is pronounced dead," says the Queen's advisor.

I nod. Of course, he is right, but I also know that he may be delaying and waiting for her to return, and I no longer care for the crown, maybe I never did. My only desire now is for peace, but I don't know if I will ever be at peace again. I do not know if anyone will accept me as Queen.

After all of this, I only feel weary. I do not know how I can smile again. Many of my people have died, and I know how they will see me now: as a brute. A murderer. A skeleton-lover. *Is there even a place for me here now? And if I do take the throne, what will that mean for me and the people?*

But, out of the darkness, one of the people walks forward through the crowd of bony figures and toward me. He is, after all, a dwarf, and his kind have been rejected for centuries, yet I am not completely abandoned.

"At your service, my lady," says the dwarf, bowing his head low.

A gnome arrives. At first, I am afraid, for I remember how I was treated in the mines. But, he lays a crystal of pure light at my feet, "Forgive us for doubting," he says.

"Rise," I say, "Go and tell the people there is nothing to fear. The mobs are not here to hurt us, and we will no longer harm them."

My advisor says, "I would not give such a message. There will be a revolt. They will hate you."

"Then, they hate me," I sing, but not in the way of control, but in the way of stating where I stand, very firmly.

He nods and walks from the room, but I know from the look in his eyes that he hates my decree as much as my people will.

"What shall I call you?" Skully asks, after the others have gone, and it is only he and I in the great room.

"Just call me Elle," I say.

"Elle," he says, "I like that."

I nod, yet I feel the overwhelm set in. I feel so inadequate. So weak when I sit on this throne that feels too big for me, a part of me is gone, and I will never get it back. The part of me that was young, naive, and free. The part of me that believed my people to be always looking out for my family. They turned against me. They hated me and were ready to have me killed. And now. Now that I am here, will the people really change?

I walk out into the garden and I reach for the Sea, letting it rise up to the castle gates, and rest there awhile and let it comfort me, swirling in the colors of purple and red and yellow and blue.

"Come, let us dance," Skully says. I feel foolish and weary, but I rest my head upon his hard chest and let him glide me around the garden, letting myself melt into him, and from somewhere in the distant trees, music begins, a serenade of currents.

Chapter Eighteen - Dance of My Bones

♥

"I've always dreamed of this moment, but I never thought it be possible," he says, and when I look up into his eyes, the eye sockets are a bright glow, so bright I have to look away, almost as bright as the stars in the night sky.

"I cannot give you what you desire," I say.

He just puts his hand up to my face, stroking the few strands from my face, and says, "No matter, child."

And so, I am like a child, letting him carry me around in circles, until the weariness starts to fade away. I am finally home, here in this skeleton's arms.

My first night in my old bed feels surreal. Skully tucks me in, as all of the servants have fled the castle, except a few whose loyalty won out over their fear of the skeletons. Still, they fear me, and I will not ask them to tend to me now.

Skully has said he will keep watch. I told him it isn't necessary, yet I am comforted knowing he is near.

I lie in my cozy bed, the comforters feeling too soft. The cushion feels like a pillow, and yet something isn't right. I feel eyes upon me, and a shiver runs down my spine, in the one place I once saw as safe. Home. This place doesn't feel like home. There is a darkness here. A lingering. *Is she still alive?*

I get up and look out the window, out onto the sprawling gardens where I grew up, romping in the wildflowers that grow there. Yet, I am changed now. The hatred is gone that I once felt for the skeletons. The fear of them is gone, too. *Now, I fear someone else, but who?*

Chapter Nineteen – Chills In The Night

♥

A draft blows in through the open window, and I stand, unmoving. Unsure what I am waiting for. When the icy chill comes in through the window, it is more than just the cool wind. It is the rule-book rising to meet me. The chains of society that I once wore, coming back to bind me once again.

"Do as you're told," it whispers.

"Who are you?" I ask.

"She who keeps Everything. As it is-to-be. Everyone in their place. Order."

"A siren's cruelty, you mean," I say, for I know what she is. She cannot hide this from me. *Is it my Mother? Or someone else? Another Siren come to attack me?*

"There is no cruelty when everyone does as they are told," says the chill. "Return to who you are to be, and everyone lives happily ever after."

"That's a lie," I scream into the dark, turning to try to find whatever it is, even though I recognize this energy and know it well. Reaching

I pull back the curtains, but only feeling its presence like a menacing cloud over me, in me, and all around me as I whirl around. It is Her. I know it, and yet I don't wish to believe it. I cradle my head in my hands. My aching head. *Why does everything hurt so?*

Eloise, I hear my name called over and over again. *Eloise, come back.* It is someone else. It is warmth to me. Light. I want to return. Return to that voice. Return to the place where he held me. Safe.

Let me go. Let. Me. Go. But I can't speak the words. I can't do anything. Nothing at all. Nothingness. I cannot even sing to protect myself now.

But I still feel. There is still some feeling left within me. "Let go. Come with me," says the chilling waters, taking shape before me. The shape of beauty. Yet, a cold beauty with hard lines and venomous lips.

"No," I say, gritting my teeth, holding my feet firmly in place. "No, no, no."

My no's are weak and unimportant. She pulls me up and away and into a place where I know nothing. There is nothing. Even the chill is gone. Even my tears and whatever I know I ought to feel is gone. What I used to call fear no longer exists. It is. I am. But also, I am not. And it is not. I am carried out to Sea, and I float for I do not know how long.

There was a name I used to say. A person or being who was my hero. But even this is gone. Memory is pulled from me like stuffing from a scarecrow.

And so it goes on. Time is timeless. Everything is meaningless. There is nothing, just as I was told. Or at least, I think I was told that this would happen. Someday.

A way out. What is that? Out where? Beyond? So tired. Can't move. Can't think, but want to. I float endlessly on the sea, and the sea envelops me, but it is not where I wish to be. I wish to be in the water that I trust. In the waves that are safe and warm.

"Are you ready to listen?" a voice says.

I know that cool presence. It wraps itself around my neck, so tight. So cold. And yet, when I look, it is the only thing of beauty here. *Can something be beautiful and also revolting and cruel?* I ask my water to come. To save me. It does come, in a rush of sparkly blue, and yet it cannot come near. Something holds it back, so that I cannot be comforted by what I need. *Does what I need mean that I am a siren? That I am just like my mother. A controlling person?*

"Listen?" I ask, even answering a simple question is difficult. Like my mind is moving ever so slowly. So, so tired.

"You are ready," says the voice, "You will do as I say, and it will be beautiful to see everything go back to how it is to be, and for them to be destroyed, once and for all."

I wake in my room. Or at least it looks like my room, but it feels gray and cold. I get up. I dress, shivering. I go to the meetings, yet I am no longer here. Not as me.

"The skeletons must be disposed of," says my advisor. "They are growing more dangerous every day."

"Yes," I say, without thought. Yet there is a wrong feeling I brush away, like cobwebs in the corners of my mind. This is so wrong, but I cannot fight it.

Only one skeleton refuses to leave. "What have ye done to her?" the skeleton screams, and it pierces something within me. There is a feeling there. The first real feeling I've felt in a long time.

"What shall I do with him?" asks the guard.

"I don't know," I say to the guard, dumbfounded by this creature. A creature I ought to hate, and yet I do not. Still, there is something else within me. A memory I reach for. A memory that tastes like honey.

"Remember love," says the skeleton, before the guard takes him away, dragging his bones across the hard floor. They make a scraping sound.

Love. That's absurd. What did the skeleton mean by this? His words are like a burning flame, and like a wave that licks at the edge of my mind.

I am disturbed as my maid brushes my hair, frazzled by the words or by the creature. Wishing I remembered what he spoke of. Wondering if I'm the one who is going crazy.

"Don't heed him, my lady," soothes my maid. "He's a little crazy in the head, as they all are."

I nod in agreement and take a deep breath. Of course. Of course.

My head aches as I retire to my room, and yet nothing satisfies me. Not the praise of my people. Not the suitors who call and bow at my feet, as if I were something more than I am. As if I am something beautiful, when I only feel ugly. I toss my things across the room, not caring when they fall and break. I run to the window and claw at the curtains. I sob into my pillow.

I find a note on my pillow that night. It is crumpled, torn, and the words are scrawled in messy writing.

Elle,

Meet me at the library at midnight on the third day,

the note reads.

I toss and turn most of the night, contemplating the message. I know myself too well. No matter how much I resist, I will go there. The note is drawing me there. To the place I once was long ago.

Am I foolish, or lonely? The next night, I barely sleep, and on the third night, I pace my room until the clock strikes half past eleven.

I walk out of my room at a quarter to twelve, down the hall, and out of the castle doors, going to the place, my feet guiding me there.

Chapter Twenty - Magic Kiss

♥

You aren't following the rules, says the chill. A cold blast of water in my face splashes me awake. Beware.

A chill I should be wary of. A chill that I know well. A chill, I fear. Where is the warm water I long for? Where has it gone? Yet, I press on, ignoring the voice, and shivering with each step in this thin nightgown. I throw on a cloak and walk a path I shouldn't know, yet it's as if someone is leading me there. I take the short path. A simple portal I know well. I step through the purple mist and I find the hidden library as the clock strikes midnight, pressing into the hidden door, and stepping inside.

"Back again?" says a small voice. I look down to discover a snail sitting on a desk, gazing up at me through tiny spectacles.

"I'm here to meet someone," I say.

"Well, just as long as you don't bring the whole king's army here," the snail grumbles.

I nod, but still, everything is foggy, as if my mind is under blankets, and I'm struggling to escape.

And yet, when the skeleton enters the room, something changes. The chill that I've felt every day disappears, and there is something in its place. Joy?

He smiles at me, "Skully knew you would come," he says.

I nod, still unsure. "Why are you so happy to see me?" I ask, suspicion and fear in my stomach.

"Because you are still alive," he says. "Skully, sad to see yer lost again."

"Yes?" I say, unsure of myself. I twist my fingers nervously.

How does he know me? Why does he care?

I take a step back. He takes a step forward.

"I don't know why I'm here. I need to get back home," I say.

"Love is the only way of return," the skeleton says.

"I don't think I can love," I say. Turning, I knock a book off the shelf. It tumbles to the floor and opens, and a glorious light spills out of the book's center.

"Don't think," the skeleton says. "Just do, Elle."

Elle? Is that my name? It sounds familiar. Yes, yes, it is.

He takes my hand, and I don't pull back, surprised at how warm his touch is. It is not darkness. It is not a human touch. It is not like anything I've known. And when I turn to look at him, he is golden, his bones illuminated by some inner light.

And for a moment, there isn't anyone else. There isn't anything else. There are only the two of us, and I am *home*.

"I am Elle, aren't I?" I say.

Skully steps forward, and before I can stop myself. Before I even know what I'm doing, I lean in to kiss him, but something is there, between us. It is She. Her beautiful face and sharp teeth, and all too perfect smile.

"You naughty girl," she says, "Kissing the dead."

She grabs the skeleton. Throws his body against the wall. His bones break apart. Falling to the floor, in a heap. Crushed. The cold comes back again, and yet this time I see it for what it is, and I reach for the book on the floor, and toss it toward her, the light pouring out and onto her, revealing her beauty for what it truly is: ugliness.

"You are the one who is dead," I say, but I am sorry to say it. I am sad to see her this way.

She screams, and it's then that I remember the magic. I rush over to the skull, and I lean down, and I kiss the hard, cold surface of where his lips ought to be, tears rushing down my face. My memories flood back faster than I can receive them, overloading my system at the speed of light.

I hear a shriek from behind me.

"This isn't the end," she cackles, as she fades and blinks in and out of view. "This is only the beginning of a new world." She blinks out of view completely.

I look down to where the pile of bones ought to be to find a young man standing before me, and when he smiles, there is the light I've known all along. His eyes are gray, with hints of gold at their center, and he wears a pirate's hat.

"What happened to Skully?" I ask.

"Love has brought him to life," says Skully, taking my hand in his. We step outside, the brilliant sunshine flows over the green hills and the flowering plants, whose color is more vibrant than I ever remember.

I walk into the city, skeletons on every side of me, walking arm in arm, flowers in their hands, and smiles on their bony faces.

"What of the skeletons?" I ask. "What will happen to them?"

"They will serve and protect," he says, "As is to be."

My people step back, some shocked and others afraid. Some hold their swords out, as if to protect themselves, others bow, and some turn to flee.

I have not escaped this world, yet maybe I will learn to overcome it. In the shadows, I glimpse The One. He smiles once, and the smile is for me. I desire to run to him. Ask him so many things. And I do run. I run and I run, until I am held in his open arms that feel like everything to me. He laughs, his laughter like the music of the Sea. I want to stay forever in his arms.

"Do we live happily ever after?" I ask.

"You will live, and that is all that is needed," he says, and I know that what he says is true. To be truly alive in love is a gift.

"You mustn't keep Skully waiting," he says.

I nod, and with an ache in my chest, I turn to go, looking at his fair face before returning to the castle, yet I know he will never leave me or forsake me.

I sit upon the throne, and I look over at the pirate at my side. He grins, a familiar twinkle in his eye. Now I have the strength I need to face the darkness within me, and the darkness about me.

Acknowledgements

♥

Thanks to God for helping me write this book.

Big thanks to my loyal beta readers: Liam Koch, Aaron Brase, and Patrick Brase.

Thanks to my editing team: Stephanie Ruf and Sigrid Brase.

About the author

Minnesota author married the milkman and lives on a dairy farm with her three boys, cows, dogs, chickens, and ducks. She will be found hanging out with dark beautiful faeries, lovely skeleton pirates, runaway princess' and any manner of quirky characters she can dream up.

If you enjoyed this book it would mean the world to Heidi if you could leave her a review on Amazon. Your feedback helps others find her books!

Also by Heidi McLynn

She has also written and published "Darlene Dragon and the Worry Monster," "Sword of Wing and Shadow," "Dream Needles," "Mallory's Miraculous Dance," and "How to Frighten A Monster."